Soraya

& the Dragon

by Salima Alikhan

illustrated by Atieh Sohrabi

"Humphrey Hatches His Eggs"
illustrated by Jennifer Naalchigar

Reycraft Books
55 Fifth Avenue
New York, NY 10003
Reycraftbooks.com

Reycraft Books is a trade imprint and trademark of Newmark Learning, LLC.

Educators and Librarians: Our books may be purchased in bulk for promotional,
educational, or business use. Please contact sales@reycraftbooks.com.

This is a work of fiction. Names, characters, places, dialogue, and incidents
described either are the product of the author's imagination or are used
fictitiously. Any resemblance to actual persons, living or dead, is
entirely coincidental.

Sale of this book without a front cover or jacket may be unauthorized. If this
book is coverless, it may have been reported to the publisher as "unsold or
destroyed" and may have deprived the author and publisher of payment.

Library of Congress Control Number: 2021902048

ISBN: 978-1-4788-7368-6

Photo Credits:
Pages 3, 25, 31, 47, 63, 77, 89, 101, 117, 129: Kris_art/Getty Images
Author photo: Sam Bond Photography
Illustrator photos courtesy of Atieh Sohrabi and W. J. Naalchigar

Printed in Dongguan, China. 8557/0521/17948
10 9 8 7 6 5 4 3 2 1

First Edition Hardcover published by Reycraft Books 2021

Reycraft Books and Newmark Learning, LLC, support diversity and
the First Amendment, and celebrate the right to read.

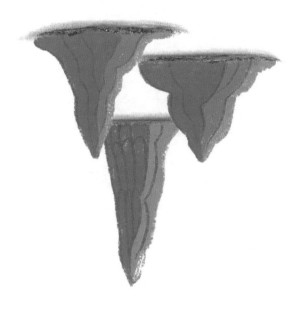

To Mindy, for befriending dragons with me. – S.A.

contents

1

Into the Mouth of the Beast

imbla Moony switched on her Blaster Belt and zoomed through space. She was on a mission to rescue a poor stray Obblegookian, who had accidentally drifted inside the enormous, yawning mouth of the fearsome Cragulon Beast.

Soraya gaped up at the entrance of Balabrook Caverns. Out of the corner of her eye, she could have sworn she glimpsed stardust and space debris floating, and maybe the swirl of a certain magic bubble cape.

Soraya held up her copy of *Nimbla Moony and the Cragulon Beast*. The cavern in front of her looked exactly like the Cragulon's huge, open mouth in the comic. Rock formations jutted up from the ground, like crooked and crowded teeth. Other formations hung from the ceiling, like fangs.

The rest of her fourth-grade class, though, didn't seem to mind that they were about to enter the mouth of a space monster.

"This is going to be the best field trip ever!" said Christoff, as the whole class crammed through the entrance.

"Are you coming, Soraya?" Ms. Staples called. "Also, what have I told you about reading and walking?"

Soraya sighed and stuffed the comic into her pocket. Too bad no one else was interested in learning about super dangerous space beasts. If they would only listen to her, she could warn them all. But *no*.

She followed her classmates inside, and immediately tripped on the uneven floor.

"Soraya, please watch where you're going."

Soraya gazed around, her jaw hanging open. The air was cool and moist, and smelled earthy. It turned out that stepping into the cavern *was* like stepping into a mouth—a mouth with huge teeth that really needed braces. But the rock formations looked like a bunch of other things, too: icicles, long strands of hair, curtains, and huge stone jellyfish. The ones poking up from the ground looked like mountains, or castle towers. A small brook gurgled through the cavern. Hidden lights shone, making the rocks seem to glow magically.

Soraya wondered if this cavern burped poisonous gas, the way the Cragulon Beast did.

"I thought this place would be boring," said Chesney, as the class gathered in the main cavern. "But it's even better than the aquarium!"

Soraya felt her awe vanish. Sadness twinged in her gut. *Nothing* could be better than the aquarium. On the class field trip there, she had met her best and only friend, a mermaid named Estelle. Estelle had been trapped in one of the aquarium tanks, and Soraya helped rescue her and return her to the sea.

Whenever Soraya thought about her friend, she felt extra lonely. Did Estelle ever think about her, too, now that she was thousands of miles away, back in her kingdom under the ocean?

"Welcome to Balabrook Caverns!" called a cavern guide. "Let's start our tour."

Soraya's class followed the guide a little farther into the mouth of the Cragulon— or, into the cavern, Soraya kept reminding herself. She stood as far away from her class as she could. Thinking about Estelle just reminded her that she had nothing in common with her classmates.

They might be excited, but none of them understood the important things—like the fact that the cavern resembled the Cragulon's mouth.

Soraya frowned as she looked around at the other kids. She knew her mom wouldn't be happy about her avoiding them. Her mom's entire mission in life seemed to be to get her to make friends. This also meant that Soraya was a constant disappointment.

Just a few months ago, right after she had come home from the aquarium trip where she'd met Estelle, her mom had said: "Did you make any friends today?"

And for the first time ever, Soraya had answered, "Yup!"

As Soraya remembered it, the conversation did not go well. Her mom dropped the apple she'd been eating. "You did? Well, we should have them over for dinner! I can call their parents to arrange it."

"You can't call her parents, Mom. She's a mermaid and she lives thousands of miles away at the bottom of the ocean, in the Mariana Trench."

Her mom's face fell.

"That's not funny, Soraya."

"I know. I'm not laughing, Mom."

Her mom pursed her lips. "You can't just hide in your comic books. You have to face real life and make real friends."

"Estelle *is* my real friend," Soraya said. "But I can't hang out with her, because she went back to the ocean. Besides, real life is overrated. Comics have heroes, magic, and adventure."

Her mom gave her a Look. "You know, we can't always just spend our time the way we *want* to, honey."

"Mom, *please.* Comics are *important* to me." Soraya didn't dare show her mom any of the comics *she'd* drawn, but she stuck *Nimbla Moony and the Jupiter Crusade* under her mom's nose.

Soraya took a deep breath and drew her head down between her shoulders. She heard herself blurting out, "I might . . . I might even want to draw my own comics. Maybe . . . someday." Soraya's eyes slid up, peeking at her mom's face.

Her mom smiled sadly. "I know you love comics. But it's important not to live in a fantasy land. You need practical goals." Her voice got faraway. "You can't live in the real world and be an artist. It's too hard. And too lonely."

"How would *you* know?" Soraya snapped. The most artistic thing she'd ever seen her mom do was use a label maker.

Something opened up in her mom's face, as if a mask had lifted. Soraya had never seen her look so sad. "I know it's hard to understand," her mom said. "The world can be harsh. I just want to protect you from that."

Soraya's legs felt like tree trunks growing roots into the carpet. She couldn't move, much less speak. Finally her mom spoke again. "Just make some real-life human friends, please, Soraya," she said, and her face closed up again.

Soraya had been thinking about that conversation all morning, especially every time she inched away from her classmates.

Her mom always acted as if Soraya could stop being weird if she wanted to—as if it were a hat that she could put on or take off. But what her mom didn't understand was that being weird was not a choice. It was just the way she was. Like being tall, or short, or having curly hair. She couldn't change it.

Soraya was the only weird one in her family. She was sure this was the reason her dad had decided to leave them a few years ago, even though her mom said that wasn't true.

Why else would someone she'd known all her life just *leave* all of a sudden?

Whenever she thought about her dad, she wanted to punch something. At the same time, she wanted to cry.

She tried to focus on the cavern. Some tourists passed by, taking pictures and pointing at the rocks. One of the formations looked like a shimmering wave. That made her remember Estelle leaping through the surf on her way home. Estelle didn't care that Soraya was weird. In fact, she liked it.

Soraya smiled a tiny smile and unclenched her fists, which had been gripping the straps of her backpack harder than she realized. It was good to know that at least one person liked her for who she really was. Even if that person was thousands of miles away under the ocean.

"The rock formations hanging from the ceiling are called *stalactites*," said the tour guide, as she pointed up at the Cragulon's fangs. "And the formations coming up from the ground are called *stalagmites*," she added. Soraya imagined the rocks pushing their way through the top and bottom of the cave like teeth through gums.

But Ms. Staples had a far more boring explanation.

"Remember what we learned, class?" she said breathlessly. Ms. Staples was so excited that she interrupted the tour guide. "These rock formations are created over thousands of years in caves made of limestone rock. Stalactites are formed when water drips from the ceiling of a cave. And *then*, the water dripping from the end of a stalactite falls to the floor of a cave, and deposits a mineral called calcite.

That's what forms a stalagmite. That's why there's often a stalagmite right under a stalactite."

The tour guide nodded, smiling. "In addition to the science, these caverns are also a place of history and legend."

Soraya snapped to attention. She stood up straight. *Legend?* Legends were her thing!

"Our most popular legend is that pirates buried treasure somewhere here in the cavern." The tour guide smiled. "But that's just an old story, of course."

Soraya got chills. She was 100 percent interested in anything involving pirates and treasure. Once, in *Nimbla Moony and the Galactic Raiders*, Nimbla Moony had battled with a pirate spaceship.

"Are there bats?" asked Phong. "Caves always have bats."

"We do have bats in the cavern, but areas where they live are off-limits to the public." The tour guide pointed behind her, toward a roped-off tunnel with a sign that said *No Admittance*. "They've been closed off to protect the bats so they won't be disturbed by visitors. But there are many other wonderful things to enjoy." She led them a little farther into the cavern. "For instance, here we have our Amazing Stalactite Organ."

There it was—a piano. Built *right into the rock*.

"Can you play that piano?" Lupita asked.

Soraya stepped closer. This was almost as interesting as buried treasure.

"This isn't exactly a piano—it's an organ," said the tour guide. "Right now it's undergoing repairs. When it's working properly, and you press the keys, they send electric signals up to rubber-tipped mallets in the ceiling.

The little hammers tap the stalactites. It makes a beautiful ringing sound."

"The stalactites look like ancient jellyfish ghosts," Soraya piped up. "So it's as if the mallets are hitting the ghost jellyfish on the tentacles."

Christoff and Naomi laughed.

"A ghost jellyfish band!" said Christoff. "I could get into that. I volunteer to be drummer!"

"Only if *I* can hit the tentacles with the mallets," said Soraya, forgetting herself.

Katie, who was in front of Soraya, turned around. She was dressed in pink, like she always was. She wore so much pink that Soraya wondered if she lived inside a bubble gum machine.

"Why are you so *weird*, Soraya?" Katie whispered. "Why can't you be *normal* for once?"

"Yeah," added Madison. Madison was Katie's meanest friend. She also copied everything

Katie did, so Soraya thought of Madison as Katie 2.0.

"If you want to stop being so weird, Soraya, you could start by not wearing rainbow pants," Katie 2.0 said.

"Rainbows are portals to other worlds," Soraya shot back. "Maybe I'll get lucky, and my rainbow pants will transport me far away from you guys."

A snort came from behind Soraya. She turned around and saw Christoff and Naomi giggling again.

Christoff said, "Good one, Soraya!"

Soraya saw that Christoff was wearing a brand-new pair of lederhosen, shorts held up by decorated suspenders. She remembered that Christoff had worn a pair of these German pants on their last field trip, and that Katie had made fun of them. Christoff didn't seem to care. Maybe he hadn't noticed.

Katie was eyeing his pants again now, her nose wrinkled.

"I like your lederhosen," Soraya said loudly, mostly to annoy Katie.

"Thanks!" said Christoff.

Katie and Madison turned back around. Their hair looked extra shiny under the dim cavern lights. Their outfits looked extra pink.

And both of them, from what Soraya could tell, had dads who loved them and often picked them up from school. Seeing that always made her stomach plunge.

Why did *other* dads stay with their kids?

Probably because those kids were normal. Probably because they paid attention in school, had shiny hair, and didn't talk about ghost jellyfish. Why couldn't parents appreciate a kid who was different, the way her friend Estelle did?

"I've always thought rainbows are portals too," Naomi whispered to Soraya.

"Same with comets," said Christoff. "I bet comets are portals."

Naomi laughed. "How can a comet be a portal? They move straight through space. A portal is a doorway into another world."

"Comets are *definitely* doorways into other worlds," said Christoff. "Soraya, want to walk with us? Maybe we can lose Katie under a stalactite."

Soraya's face flamed red. She was glad it was too dark for anyone to tell.

"I can stick up for myself," she said, inching away from them. "I can deal with Katie on my own."

Christoff blinked. "What? This isn't about Katie. We just wanted to know if you want to hang out with us."

Soraya turned away, her face still hot. "That's okay. You don't have to."

Christoff and Naomi wandered away, looking confused.

Soraya took her *Nimbla Moony* comic out of her pocket and stuffed it back into her backpack. Christoff and Naomi might *think* they wanted to hang out with her. But once they got to know her better, they'd realize she was the kind of person who'd made even her own dad want to leave.

"Time to go farther into the cavern," the tour guide announced. "Please don't touch the rock formations."

Soraya waited until her class had filed out of the room.

Then, she inched over to the Amazing Stalactite Organ. The organ did look a lot like a piano, except it had four keyboards, one stacked on top of the other.

21

She reached her hand out to push a key. A voice behind her whispered, "Are you coming, Soraya?"

She whirled around, holding back a scream. But it was just Naomi and Christoff, staring up at her.

"In a minute." Soraya frowned and put her hands behind her back. "I just want to check out the organ. Are you going to tell on me?"

"No, we were just worried when you didn't come with the class," said Naomi.

"Well, I'm fine," said Soraya.

"Okay." Naomi shrugged, and she and Christoff left to join the class. A minute later Soraya couldn't hear her classmates' voices anymore.

She turned her attention back to the organ, her heart pounding. She almost didn't care if they did tell on her. This was the most incredible instrument she'd ever seen. The keys were golden in the dim light. Nimbla Moony would compose an entire opera on this organ.

She paused. Her dad wouldn't like that she wasn't doing what she was supposed to be doing.

Well, he wasn't here, was he? She set her jaw and pressed a key. That key must not have been one of the ones that needed repairs, because a soft sound echoed through the room. Chills tingled through her. She pressed another key.

This time, Soraya heard a different sound—a low, rumbling scrape. The sound came from the roped-off passage that read *No Admittance*. She tiptoed over for a closer look. Beyond the sign, the tunnel sloped downward, a ramp into the darkness.

At the end of *that*, a stone door creaked open. Then the rumbling stopped.

Soraya's heart beat quicker. Nimbla Moony's favorite saying was *"Adventure calls, but you have to be listening!"* Soraya listened for adventure all day, every day. She sometimes listened for it so hard it made her head hurt, and made her forget to eat breakfast.

This was a call to adventure if she'd ever seen one!

Soraya slipped under the rope and hurried down the passage toward the door.

The Lair

There was only one light in the passage, midway down the long ramp. Soraya took out her penlight— a handy little thing Nimbla Moony always had with her as well. Except Nimbla's penlight was way cooler because it also turned into a blaster. Soraya's was just a waterproof pen with a top she could twist, which made it shine a light—but it was a surprisingly bright light.

She slowed down as she got closer to the bottom of the ramp.

The huge, thick, heavy stone door stood open. It looked as though it had been disguised in the rock of the cave wall, as if a chunk of the stone had just swung outward.

Warmth and a flicker of light came from behind it.

She was sure that striking the organ keys had made this door open. But how was that possible? And who else knew about this secret?

Soraya took a breath and slipped through.

And caught herself right before she walked any farther. She gasped and pressed her back against the rock. She was inside an enormous, dimly lit cavern room. A torch flickered on a bracket in the wall. The floor was piled with bright, glittering things that looked like jewels.

But that wasn't the crazy part. The crazy part was that, in the middle of the room—on *top* of the biggest pile of glittering things—there was a dragon.

An actual, real-life . . . *dragon.*

The dragon shifted on the pile of treasure. Soraya heard herself whimper. He was huge, scaly, and some shade of green. It was hard to tell exactly in the dim light. He was curled up, his wings folded over him like a blanket. Little puffs of smoke rose from the dragon's snout with every breath.

She tried to remember everything she could about dragons, but her heart was beating too hard to focus. She managed to remember that they breathed fire. Of course. No wonder it was so warm in here.

Soraya inched back toward the door. The brave thing to do would be to run and warn the cavern guides. They should know that a bloodthirsty *dragon* was behind this secret door.

She hesitated. Estelle, who made friends with everyone, would try to make friends with this dragon, too. But Soraya knew better. Dragons killed people and burned up cities, and were just generally not very nice.

Nimbla Moony would challenge this dragon. She'd swoop in and fight him. Nimbla Moony had, in fact, fought many rare space dragons. She beat them every time.

Soraya didn't have powers like Nimbla. But if this dragon was waiting here to attack people, she had a duty to defend them.

She crept along the edge of the wall to get a better look at him.

What would Nimbla do?

Use your brain, she imagined Nimbla saying.

Maybe she could trap him in here somehow. Then everyone would be safe from the dragon.

She squinted at the other side of the room and saw a wide, open tunnel passage. She could seal off that passage somehow. Then she'd sneak back out the way she'd come, and block the door behind her. That might do the trick.

Nimbla would be proud.

Of course, Soraya had no idea how she'd seal off that passage. But she had to try.

She inched across the floor of the huge cave, shaking. She was just *feet away from a dragon*. He looked oddly peaceful, snoring away, smoke drifting from his huge nostrils. But she knew he could open his mouth any second and roast her like a chicken.

She tiptoed around the dragon's treasure. She could see it more clearly now. She had expected jewels and gold, like a regular dragon's hoard. Instead, she saw notebooks with glittery covers, sparkly pens and pencils, key chains, and colorful metal water bottles.

Her eyebrows knit together. What was a dragon doing lying on top of a bunch of school supplies?

Suddenly there was a sound like a freight train, and a massive *whoosh* all around her. She clapped her hands to her ears.

A yawn. The dragon . . . was awake!

Humphrey

Soraya froze. She froze so completely she thought she'd turned into a stalagmite herself.

The dragon's huge wings unfolded. He stretched them and yawned again. He blinked open one golden eye and looked down at her.

"Are you a dream?" he asked. Then his ears drooped. "No, don't tell me. I'll be sad if you are."

The dragon opened his other eye.

Now, two enormous golden eyes were gazing down at her.

Soraya's throat felt dry. Her voice was at its very croakiest. "Why do you think I'm a dream?"

He sighed a long, sad sigh, and a gust of heat blasted through the cavern. "Because sometimes, I dream about people coming to visit me. But then I wake up and they're not really here, and I get sad."

"Well, I'm not a dream. I'm real." Soraya felt herself unfreezing just a fraction of an inch. "Can I ask you a question? Why are you sitting on a pile of school supplies instead of treasure?"

The dragon looked around as if noticing his hoard for the first time. "Oh, this *is* my treasure. These are mementos."

"What's a memento?"

"It's like a keepsake. It's something a person gives you to remember them by. When kids come visit me, they leave me little presents."

Soraya froze right back up again. "*Kids* come visit you? Real ones, that aren't dreams?"

He nodded, but his ears drooped again. "Yes. Real kids come visit me when they are on school trips. It's the kids who don't listen to their teachers, and sneak away to play that organ. It opens the secret door to this cave. The cavern guides don't know about it, of course." He sighed again. "The kids come talk to me, but then they always have to go."

Soraya gulped. "Are you sure you don't eat the kids after you meet them?"

The dragon's ears jerked up. "*Eat* them?" His golden eyes filled with tears. "I would never *eat* them. What do you think I *am*?"

Then he started to cry. He sniffled and snuffled and gulped.

Soraya unfroze all the way. "But what are you *doing* down here? How did you get here?"

The dragon wiped his eye with a huge claw. "I was born here, and I lived here with my parents for a few days when I was a tiny baby. But then some dragon hunters came. I was too small to travel, but my parents had to flee. They hid me and left me with their friends the cave bats, who said they'd watch over me until my parents could come back. The bats took great care of me. They became my family. But then . . ."

Tears swam in his huge golden eyes again. "A few years ago, I wandered out of the bat area to explore the cavern. While I was out, the cavern guides went in and sealed off the bat area, to protect the bats from tourists. I couldn't find my way back."

"Eventually I found this cavern," the dragon continued. "It was the only place big enough for me to hide. The pirates left a torch, and I lit it so that I could see. But soon, I got so big I couldn't leave here even if I wanted to. And all this time . . ." He wiped away another tear. "I've been wondering where my parents are. Have you seen them?"

Soraya had to shake her head.

"But why haven't they come back for me?" the dragon said.

Soraya felt a lump in her throat. He was asking her like she was supposed to know. She sat down, fighting the lump.

"I don't know," she said softly. "Sometimes parents just go away and you don't know why."

The dragon lowered his huge head. "I wish they'd hurry and come back. I miss them."

She hesitated for a second, then said, "I know what it's like to miss someone. My dad left me and my mom, too. He—he never calls or visits me. And my mom thinks I'm weird."

She took a big breath. It was hard to say it out loud. Estelle was the only person she'd ever told about her dad.

The dragon trained one of his big, sorrowful eyes on her. "Oh my. I'm so sorry. It's awful to miss people. If I ever meet your dad, I'll tell him to visit you."

Soraya's chest squeezed. "What about you? How often do people visit you?"

The dragon gazed toward the tunnel entrance. "Well, every few months, a kid finds me and talks to me for a while. That helps. And they always promise not to tell the cavern guides about me."

Soraya did something she couldn't have imagined just ten minutes ago, and patted the dragon's snout. She pulled her hand back fast though, because his scales were very hot.

Soraya stood up and poked around some of the dragon's mementos. She wondered how many kids had been here, and if any of them had tried to help the dragon.

"Do you have a name?" she said. "I'm Soraya."

"Hi, Soraya," said the dragon. He put his huge head back on his front legs. "I'm Humphrey. I'm glad you found me. There's nothing like having company."

Soraya thought about how she couldn't stand company, most of the time. It always felt like a chore to hang out with people.

Again, she felt a lump in her throat. She realized she probably *would* want company if she had been alone for years. She wondered if Humphrey's parents were still out there somewhere. What if the dragon hunters had found them?

Or, what if they'd left and decided they were better off without him, and hadn't come back on purpose? She felt a rush of anger. Did even *dragons* leave their own kids behind?

"Did your parents leave you any clues about where they went?" Soraya asked.

"I don't think so. Do *you* think they did?"

"Maybe." Soraya wandered around among Humphrey's hoard, poking at the items. Most of it was school-supply stuff. But she realized some of it wasn't. Every once in a while she came across something that looked very old, buried amid the other stuff.

There were a few rusted cups, discolored with age. There was also a big, tarnished brass buckle. Curious, she picked up something at the very bottom of the pile.

Her heart beat faster. It was a large gold coin. She knew what kind of coin this was—a doubloon. And doubloons belonged to . . . *pirates.*

Her heart still pounding, she picked up an old brass tube. The end of the tube screwed off. As soon as she opened it, a rolled-up piece of paper slid out.

Soraya unrolled the paper. It was old and crinkly. There were pictures and symbols all over it, as well as some writing.

Butterflies zoomed around in her stomach. "Humphrey!"

"What?"

"I think this is a treasure map!"

"*What?*" Humphrey's eyes went wide.

"This paper is a map of the cavern. It says there's treasure buried here! There's an *X* here, for *X* marks the spot. There's even a drawing of a treasure chest."

Humphrey waddled over to her. His hoard crunched and cascaded underneath him. "That old metal tube?" He looked dumbfounded. "That was already here when I got here."

"So why didn't you open it?" she said.

He sighed. "I don't have any thumbs. Try opening a lid without thumbs."

"Well," said Soraya, "the cavern guide said that pirates buried treasure in this cave. They must have left this map."

Humphrey squinted at the map, studying it. Then two puffs of smoke shot from his nostrils. "I think this map leads back to the bat area, where my friends are!"

Humphrey went on, "The bats are in the biggest part of the caverns, on the eastern side. The *X* marks the spot right there!"

Soraya jumped up and down. "So this *X* tells us where the bats are, *and* where the treasure is? We have to get there. We can use the map!"

"It would be great to see my bat family again," Humphrey said. "Do you think the bats might know where my dragon parents are?"

"I don't know." Soraya didn't want to give Humphrey false hope. She didn't have much faith in parents who walked out on their kids. "But just think, if we find the bats, you'll have company again!"

Humphrey was so excited that he tried to jump up and down, but all he could manage to do was trample his school supplies. So instead he spun in circles a few times, which meant Soraya had to jump over his giant tail so it wouldn't knock her over.

Then suddenly he stopped short, his ears drooping. "I forgot. I'm too big." He nodded at the tunnel opening across the room. "I definitely can't get through the door you came through. There's another tunnel over there. I can fit inside the tunnel itself, but I don't fit into any of the openings leading off it. I've tried."

"We'll figure something out." Soraya rolled up the map, stuffed it back into the tube, and slid the tube into her backpack. "But you can't stay here all alone. We *have* to follow this treasure map."

She felt in her bones that this was the right thing to do. One did not just ignore a lonely friend who'd been abandoned by his parents. Also, one did not just ignore a treasure map. Nimbla Moony would for *sure* follow this map. As a matter of fact, in *Nimbla Moony and the Great Space Caper*, Nimbla had buried some treasure and drawn a map herself.

"Come on," Soraya said. "We're leaving."

"But what about my mementos?" Humphrey glanced around at his hoard.

Soraya thought for a moment. "We can't take them all, but I can fit a few in my backpack."

Humphrey mumbled to himself as he pawed through the pile of school supplies. Finally, he used his mouth to pick up a notebook, a pencil case with a sunflower on it, a rainbow key chain, and a tennis ball. He dropped them gently at Soraya's feet. They were covered in his spit.

"Do you think the other kids will be mad that I didn't take *their* mementos, too?" he said.

Soraya stuffed the things he had picked into her backpack, trying to ignore the spit.

"The kids will understand," she said firmly, and led the way to the tunnel opening across the room. "They would want you to get back to the bats so that you're not lonely anymore."

"Okay," Humphrey said, waddling after Soraya. "I hope they know I'll never forget them."

Drool to the Rescue

Humphrey was right: he could fit (barely) into the tunnel leading out of the room. He had to keep his head low. Wisps of smoke puffed from his snout as he waddled along. All the openings leading off the tunnel were too small for him.

Soraya noticed that something green and slimy was dripping out of Humphrey's mouth. It was pretty gross. She bit her lip, not wanting to hurt his feelings, but she couldn't help staring. It swung like a pendulum.

"I drool when I get nervous," Humphrey whispered. A glob of drool plopped onto the ground.

Soraya made a face, but made sure he didn't see. She took out her penlight and consulted the map. Then she examined all the tunnel mouths that opened off the passage they were in. There were at least eight of them.

"The map says we need to take this third tunnel on the left," she said.

Humphrey drooled some more. "I won't fit."

Soraya's heart sank. Humphrey was right, of course.

"Maybe I could just go and see if I can find help—" Soraya began.

"No!" Humphrey said. "Don't leave me!"

"Okay, okay," Soraya promised. "I won't."

"Maybe I could back into the tunnel opening?" Humphrey said.

Soraya bit her lip. "I don't know . . ."

But Humphrey had already spun around. He folded his wings up as tight as they would go. Then he backed himself, tail first, into the tunnel. He looked hopeful. He scooted backward—and then let out a low moan.

"I'm stuck!"

"Okay. *Don't panic*," said Soraya. But on the inside, *she* was panicking. She was the one who'd gotten him into this mess. "We'll figure something out. Just stay there and let's think."

Humphrey wasn't going anywhere. His head and forelegs stuck out of the tunnel, and he was drooling more than before.

What would Nimbla Moony do? Soraya stomped her foot in frustration. The problem was that annoying things like this *never* slowed down Nimbla Moony. She would already have blasted open the tunnels with her penlight blaster.

Suddenly Humphrey lifted his head and sniffed. "What's that noise? And smell?"

"What smell?" said Soraya. "What noise? I don't hear anything."

"Dragons have excellent hearing. And sense of smell. Someone's coming."

Soraya froze up again. He was right. She could hear it now, too. Someone was coming from the direction of Humphrey's cave.

"Someone found the open door!" she said.

"We're done for!" said Humphrey, whimpering.

A voice came from back in the cavern room where Soraya had found Humphrey. "Soraya? Are you here?"

Soraya paused. She knew that voice.

"Stay here," she whispered to Humphrey, and darted back down the tunnel.

"Where would I go?" said Humphrey.

Soraya skidded into the room just as Naomi and Christoff appeared behind Humphrey's pile of mementos.

"*Soraya?*" said Christoff, wide-eyed. "What *is* all this?"

"It looks like a bunch of school supplies, and some other really old stuff," said Naomi.

"What are you *doing* here?" Soraya demanded.

"We were worried about you," Naomi said, tripping over a pile of notebooks. "When you didn't join the rest of the class, we went back and saw you go down into that restricted tunnel. We waited to see if you'd come out again. When you didn't, we followed."

"Well, there's nothing down here," Soraya said, glancing toward the tunnel. "You need to go back."

Naomi gulped and glanced at Christoff.
"Well . . . I don't know if we can," she said.
"Christoff leaned on a notch in the wall after
we came in, and that stone door shut behind
us. We tried to figure out how to open it, but
we couldn't."

Soraya's heart thumped. What was she
going to do now? If they were trapped in here,
the cavern guides would find Humphrey for
sure. Who knew what they would do to him?

She shook her head and sighed heavily. "That's *not* how Nimbla Moony would have done it. Zero stealth."

Christoff's face fell. "You mean the comic-book superhero? And I didn't do it on purpose." Then his head snapped up. "What's *that*?"

He pointed behind Soraya. She whirled around and saw a puff of smoke drift in from the tunnel.

"It's nothing," she said quickly.

Naomi sniffed the air. "Is something burning down here?"

"No!" said Soraya, but it was too late.

Christoff and Naomi dashed into the tunnel. Soraya followed, her heart racing so hard she felt light-headed.

She almost bumped into Naomi and Christoff. They had both stopped in their tracks, and were staring at Humphrey's enormous front half sticking out of the tunnel.

Humphrey stared back at them, drooling so much there was now a small river in the passage.

Naomi screamed.

"*Ssshhhhh!*" Soraya hissed. She knew she should probably be nicer, but Naomi and Christoff were going to ruin everything.

Christoff pointed at Humphrey. His voice was just as squeaky as Soraya's had been when she'd first seen the dragon. "What is *that*?"

"I thought I would fit," Humphrey said with a shrug.

Christoff staggered backward. "It *talks*?"

Soraya stood in front of Humphrey protectively. "Listen," she said. "His name is Humphrey and he's been stuck down here for a while. He's harmless, so you *can't tell on him.*" She wanted to add that all he was doing was waiting for his parents, but the lump formed in her throat again. She would *not* let Humphrey get hurt any more than he already had been.

Christoff shook his head as if he could clear his vision that way. "It's a dragon . . . *who talks.*"

"Yeah." As quickly as she could, trying to talk around the lump, Soraya told them Humphrey's story.

After several minutes, Christoff and Naomi relaxed. Maybe it was because poor Humphrey looked so sad and pathetic, stuck there.

Christoff's knees were shaking, but he rubbed his eyes and asked Humphrey, "So you're not going to burn us alive?"

Humphrey looked offended. "I don't burn people."

"I've always wanted to meet a dragon," Naomi said. "Can I—can I touch your scales? Or would that be rude?"

"Sure," Humphrey said, sighing. "It's too bad you can only see the front half of me. I'm much more impressive when you can see my wings, too."

Naomi smiled weakly. She looked a little shaky, too.

Soraya bristled. *She* had found Humphrey; he was *her* friend. And now Christoff and Naomi were acting as if they were suddenly his buddies too.

Christoff turned to Soraya, though still keeping an eye on Humphrey. "You said you're following a treasure map?"

"Yes." Soraya backed up a step. "I'm getting Humphrey out of here. So he can be with the bats again."

"But now he's stuck. So you can't go anywhere until he's *un*-stuck." Naomi stepped right into a puddle of Humphrey's drool. "Ew."

"He can't help it," Soraya said. "He drools when he's nervous."

"So why don't we just try to push him as hard as we can?" said Christoff. "See if we can get him through?"

Soraya narrowed her eyes. "Why do you want to help?"

"Because he obviously needs help," Christoff said. He sounded annoyed. "And it's a nice thing to do to help people. Or dragons."

Soraya flushed. "Okay."

She really didn't want anyone's help, but she'd probably need it to get Humphrey through the tunnel entrance.

"First," said Naomi, "we need to be able to see better." She fished a flashlight out of her backpack, turned it on, and leaned it against the wall so that it lit up the space.

"Is that one of those flashlights that light up different colors?" Soraya said.

"Yeah!" said Naomi. "I always keep it with me, just in case."

"Those look like laser blasters to me, almost as cool as the ones Nimbla Moony has," said Soraya.

Naomi beamed.

"Ready, Humphrey?" The three of them braced against the dragon's scaly chest. They pushed with all their might, but poor Humphrey didn't budge an inch.

"I'll just be stuck here forever," he said, drooping his big head. "I'll grow into an old dragon, stuffed into a tunnel entrance."

"You are *not* going to stay stuck," Soraya said. "We'll figure this out."

But she was starting to get scared. She'd just admitted to Christoff and Naomi that she'd told Humphrey to leave his cave. And now, because of her, he was stuck. Were they going to hate her for that?

Naomi wandered back over to the puddle of drool. Then she studied Humphrey. "We've been doing it the wrong way. What we need is something slippery."

Naomi looked excited. She walked closer to Humphrey. Soraya could hardly believe it, but Naomi *grabbed a handful of his drool.* "How much drool do you think you can produce, Humphrey?"

His eyes got big. "Probably a lot. I'm really scared right now."

"Okay, good. Go ahead and drool as much as you can. And, you two," Naomi said, turning to Soraya and Christoff. "Help me."

She scooped up more of Humphrey's slimy drool. She climbed onto his foreleg, then his shoulder, and up to his back. She crawled down his back to the tunnel entrance where he was stuck, and started rubbing the drool all over his scales.

"Come *on*, guys," Naomi said. Soraya and Christoff were watching her with their mouths open in horror.

Christoff took a deep breath. "Okay. I'll just pretend it's not drool." He took a handful of the stuff himself, wrinkled his nose, and clambered up onto Humphrey's back.

"Pretend it's lava from a volcano monster," said Soraya. "That makes it easier."

Christoff laughed as he smeared drool over Humphrey. "I'm not sure that's better. But I'll try."

Humphrey was taking his assignment to drool so seriously that it looked as if the tunnel might flood any second. Soraya scooped up some drool. Trying not to gag, she joined Naomi and Christoff. They slathered the drool all over the dragon's back, trying to get it as slimy as possible.

"That should do it." Naomi slid off his back.

"Now see if you can wiggle backward bit by bit, Humphrey. It should be easier now."

Humphrey cautiously wriggled back—first one step, then another. He squeezed his eyes shut with effort.

And then, suddenly . . . *POP!* He made it through.

Hotter than a Million Ovens

H umphrey looked so surprised that he tried to jump, but bumped his head on the ceiling. "Ow!" he said. Then he smiled. "Hey, I got *through*!"

Drool dripped off his sides, and he looked a little dazed, but Soraya was pretty sure there had never been a happier dragon.

Naomi beamed and wiped her drool-covered hands on her pants. "So, where to next? What does the map say?"

"What do you mean?" said Soraya nervously.

"Don't we need to get Humphrey back to the bats before the field trip is over?" said Christoff.

"We only have two hours," Naomi added. "That's when our class is meeting at the gift shop."

Naomi and Christoff looked hopefully at Soraya.

Soraya shifted from foot to foot. She didn't want other people taking over her adventure. Especially people who felt sorry for her.

Then Estelle's voice popped into her head: *It's okay to ask for help, Soraya. We all need friends.*

Soraya crossed her arms. Just because Naomi and Christoff were helping didn't mean they wanted to be her friends. They probably just wanted to be part of a dragon adventure.

Who wouldn't want that?

Christoff could see that Soraya was hesitating. "It looks like you guys could use help," he said. "Plus, we can't go back the other way."

He did have a point about not being able to go back the other way. After all, Christoff had accidentally sealed the door.

Reluctantly, Soraya pulled out the map and showed it to them. Christoff raised his eyebrows as he studied it. "Wow. You can tell this map is really old. And a lot of the stuff on here isn't on the official cavern maps. I don't think the guides know about some of these tunnels."

Soraya perked up, forgetting her reluctance for a second. She liked secret tunnels almost as much as she liked dragons. And outer space.

Naomi turned to Christoff. "How do you know so much about what's in these caverns?"

"I read all about Balabrook Caverns before the field trip," said Christoff. "So I know a lot about them." He pointed at the map. "It says to go through a tunnel here, but I know for a fact this tunnel is not on the official cavern maps."

Soraya sighed. It seemed as if she might need Christoff's and Naomi's help after all. Unlike Christoff, she didn't know the first thing about caverns, not unless you counted Nimbla Moony's adventures blowing them up. And Naomi seemed to be really good at solving problems—it had been a great idea to use Humphrey's drool to get him unstuck from the tunnel.

"Fine, you can come," she said, rolling up the map.

"Friends!" said Humphrey, puffing smoke from his nostrils. He'd stopped drooling, for now. "This is more friends than I've had in a long time!"

Soraya patted his leg. "Once we get you back to your bat family, you'll have lots of friends again."

She still wasn't convinced that Naomi and Christoff wanted to be friends, but the most important thing was to help Humphrey. Soraya told herself it didn't matter if the other kids ended up liking her or not.

Humphrey folded his wings up tight, and they all trundled down the tunnel. From somewhere far above, a tiny sliver of light shined so that the cavern was very faintly illuminated.

"Some of these unmarked parts of the cave might not be that far underground . . . there are probably cracks above us, letting in light," Christoff said.

Soon, they came to another passage.

Soraya tensed up. This one looked too small for Humphrey, too.

"Oh *no*," he groaned. "Is this just going to keep happening? I don't know if I have much drool left right now. And my sonic blasts are no good."

"Your *sonic blasts*?" said Soraya. "What are you talking about?"

Humphrey blushed. "My adoptive bat parents tried to teach me to do echolocation, the way they do. But it went horribly wrong. Just another thing I'm not good at."

"Echo-lo-*what*?" said Soraya.

"Echolocation is how bats find things in the dark," said Naomi.

Humphrey nodded forlornly. "Yeah. Bats are really good at it. They shoot out sound waves. When those waves hit the objects around them, they bounce back, so the bats know where the objects are. My bat family tried to teach me how to do it, but it turns out it's *very* different when a dragon tries it. I almost destroyed the cavern because my sound waves were so strong. I haven't tried it since." He hung his head. "So embarrassing."

He looked as though he was about to cry. Soraya patted his side.

"There have to be other options," Naomi said after a thoughtful pause. "There must be things you are especially *good* at, too. Do you ever breathe fire, Humphrey? I mean, besides lighting your torch?"

Humphrey's eyes got huge. "I would *never*! What if I burn someone?"

"I'm not asking if you *would*. I'm asking if you *could*," said Naomi. "How hot is dragon fire?"

"Hotter than a million ovens." Humphrey looked ill. "But, um . . . we have several heat levels."

"What does that mean?"

"That means we can choose whether we want to blow hot, very hot, or *super* hot. The lowest heat level is smolder. That's mostly for cooking meals."

"What's 'smolder'?" said Christoff.

"I like that word," said Soraya. "But I don't know what it means either."

"It means burning slowly, without flames," said Naomi.

Humphrey nodded. "That's right. Then there's the melt level. The hottest is the fire-blast level." He shrank back. "But I'd *never* use that."

Soraya watched, slightly uncomfortable. She wondered if Naomi's dad was proud of her for all the science she knew. He probably was. According to her mom, science was way more useful than all the stuff Soraya liked.

"What does the fire-blast level do?" asked Christoff.

"I shoot a huge ball of fire and it blasts things apart," Humphrey said in a small voice. "At least, I think it will. I've never tried it before."

"You don't need to use the fire-blast level," said Naomi. "It sounds like your fire can melt most things. Maybe you can use the melt level to melt the edges of this passage. Just enough to widen it so that you can get through."

Humphrey's eyes grew huge. "You want me to melt the *rock*?"

"Yup," said Naomi.

"But you should be careful," Soraya warned, glad to be able to add something to the conversation. "If you make it through that passage, there might be a booby trap on the other side."

Everyone turned around and looked at her.

"What's a booby trap?" said Humphrey.

"Booby traps are obstacles that pirates create to make sure people don't find their treasure," Soraya explained. "From everything I've read, pirates are pretty creative with their booby traps."

Humphrey's green scales paled.

"The important thing is getting through first, Humphrey," said Naomi. "So go ahead and try your melt level."

Humphrey faced the passage and screwed his eyes shut. Sparks flew out of his mouth and landed on the edges of the passage, which turned a fiery red. The tunnel got very hot. Soraya, Naomi, and Christoff backed away, sweating. The rock melted, little by little. Soon it was just wide enough to let Humphrey through.

But no one moved. It was so hot that Soraya had to turn her back. Embers and bits of smoldering rock fell from the passage. Smoke billowed into their noses.

"Whoa," said Christoff, gasping and wiping sweat from his face. "Way to go, Humphrey!"

Humphrey danced his little trampling happy dance. "Did you *see* that? I did it!"

"I can't breathe," said Naomi, her eyes watering.

Soraya bent over coughing. "It's still not safe to go through, though. We'll get burned."

Humphrey bit his lip. "Hurry," he said. "Get under my wings!"

He extended his wings just wide enough for them to huddle underneath, and they all squeezed through the passage. Once they were through, they kept scooting forward, until the air was clear of smoke.

"I can *breathe* again," said Naomi.

Soraya took great big gulps of air, too. They were in a pitch-dark space now that seemed bigger than where they'd been before. She could hear echoes.

"I wonder where we are," she said, pulling out her penlight.

Just as she managed to turn it on, Humphrey pushed through the tunnel behind them—and she realized they'd all been standing on a narrow ledge.

And that now, they were all tumbling off.

An Underground Lake

They landed in cold water that closed over Soraya's head. She paddled furiously until she was back up above the surface, gasping and sputtering.

Treading water, she waved around her trusty penlight. Thank goodness it was waterproof. Naomi and Christoff bobbed up near her, and Naomi switched on her flashlight, too.

They were in a huge underground lake.

Humphrey paddled frantically next to Soraya, splashing so hard she could barely see.

"I can't swim," he said, gasping.

"Can't you just stand up in the water?" asked Christoff.

"It's too deep," said Humphrey. "I can't touch the bottom!"

"Don't panic—we'll teach you how to swim," Soraya told him.

"Here, I'll show you." Naomi swam over to him. "Paddle your front and back legs—yes, just like that—and keep your head above water. Good. Now try to push forward through the water . . . that's it . . ."

Still treading water, Soraya turned her attention to the ceiling.

The stalactites here were longer and sharper than the other ones she'd seen. Some of them reached almost all the way to the surface of the water.

"There's another tunnel over there," said Naomi, pointing. Across from them, on the other side of the lake, was an opening in the wall.

"We've only got to swim over there—it's not that far," Christoff said. "You can do it, Humphrey."

"Wait!" said Soraya. "We might not be able to just swim to the other side. This could be part of a booby trap."

She was feeling a little more confident pointing out these things; so far, neither Naomi nor Christoff had laughed at her.

Now Christoff looked nervous. "So what do we do?"

"We go very slowly, and keep our eyes open."
Carefully, Soraya paddled forward.

Humphrey's eyes were wide with fear, but at least he was staying above water now. "It's getting a little easier," he said.

Naomi nodded encouragingly. "Just think of it as dragon paddling."

The four of them started slowly swimming across the lake.

Splash! Just then, a stalactite fell from the ceiling and into the water. It cut the surface like a knife.

Humphrey roared in terror. He splashed backward, beating his wings against the water.

"I knew it," said Soraya. "This lake *is* booby-trapped. That wasn't an accident. Be careful—don't move!"

They all treaded water, holding their breath and staring at the ceiling.

"We can't just tread water forever," whispered Christoff.

But as soon as they started swimming again, two more stalactites fell. They sliced the water like daggers.

Humphrey howled. "We're going to get skewered like shish kebabs!"

"Humphrey, keep treading water," Soraya said, but it was useless. He was splashing more frantically than ever.

"I say we wait to see if they're falling in a pattern," said Naomi.

"I say we swim for the other side as fast as we can," said Christoff.

"I agree with Christoff," said Soraya.

The four of them started swimming again, this time as quickly as they could.

Stalactites rained down on them from all directions.

"Oww!" wailed Humphrey.

"Are you okay?" Soraya asked.

He wiggled his head. His eyes looked a little crossed. "Yeah. One of them hit me on the head. But dragon skulls are pretty hard."

Soraya knew that she, Naomi, and Christoff wouldn't be as lucky if a stalactite fell on them. She swam faster, struggling to hold up her penlight. "Come on, guys!"

She glanced back. Humphrey was glaring at the ceiling.

"Watch this," he said. As soon as another stalactite fell, he opened his mouth and blasted it with fire. The stalactite melted before it hit the water, turning into a sizzling stream of goo.

"*That's* the fire-blast level," said Humphrey, smiling. "I figure it's safe to use it in here, since the water will put out the fire."

The ceiling trembled. Several more stalactites fell.

"Hey—the water's getting hot," Naomi said, splashing around. "That melted stalactite was like pouring lava into this lake, Humphrey!"

She was right—the water was suddenly warm.

"We'd better hurry," said Soraya.

The four of them plunged and paddled as fast as they could. Every once in a while, a terrific crack sounded, as Humphrey blasted and melted another stalactite. The water was getting hotter and hotter. Heat hit Soraya's legs in waves.

Just then, a stalactite dropped from directly above Naomi. She tried to leap out of the way, but it speared her backpack—and dragged her under the water.

"Naomi!" Christoff and Soraya screamed at the same time.

"I was afraid if I melted that one, it would hit Naomi!" Humphrey said, paddling toward them. "I'm sorry."

"I'll get her." Christoff dove down in the spot where Naomi had disappeared.

Soraya watched the dark water close over him, trying not to think about how hot the lake was now. It was like the hottest bath she'd ever taken. She felt helpless, treading water and holding up her penlight. If it went out, they wouldn't be able to see anything at all.

"You've got to keep the other stalactites from falling on them, Humphrey," she said.

Humphrey floundered around, batting away stalactites with his wings as they fell. He didn't dare use his fire. He missed one of the stalactites, which came so close that when it hit the lake, water splashed up into Soraya's face and blinded her for a second.

Next to her, Christoff surfaced, dragging Naomi behind him.

"So hot," she said, gasping for breath. "Almost had to leave my backpack behind."

She was coughing and sputtering, but otherwise looked okay. She still had her flashlight, too.

Soraya let out a sigh of relief.

"That was pretty brave, Christoff," she said.

"Thanks," he said, coughing. "Humphrey kept us safe too. Now let's go!"

They paddled frantically the rest of the way across the lake, narrowly missing more falling stalactites.

Naomi was the first of them to reach the other side. She climbed up onto the ledge in front of the tunnel, dripping. She looked very eager to get out of there. But the tunnel entrance was filled with boulders.

"Come on, Humphrey," she called. "You'll have to open this passage too, before the whole ceiling comes down on us!"

"It's too hot in here for him to use his fire," Soraya pointed out. "I feel like I'm going to burn to death."

"What about that sonic blast thing?" said Christoff.

"Oh no," Humphrey said, whimpering as he lumbered up onto the ledge. Christoff and Soraya scrambled up after him. "I might kill us all if I try the sonic blast."

Above the ledge, the ceiling rumbled and shook. "Well, we have to try something," said Christoff.

"You can do it, Humphrey," said Soraya. "Think sonic thoughts."

Humphrey nodded, and screwed up his eyes in concentration. "Take cover," he warned.

Soraya clung to the wall; she had no idea what was going to happen.

Humphrey's eyes flew wide open and so did his mouth. The rock in front of them blasted apart, making a thunderous sound. Soraya covered her face as bits of rock blew past her. The sound seemed to have dislodged the rest of the stalactites. They started to rain down.

"Go, go, go!" said Soraya. She and the others leapt forward through the hole Humphrey had made, just as a stalactite the size of a tree trunk hit the ground where she'd been standing a second before.

Cave Music

Everyone stood in the tunnel, panting as they tried to catch their breaths. Naomi turned on her flashlight. Soraya took off her backpack and poured out the water. She checked the map and let out a sigh of relief. Luckily, it was still dry. The brass tube seemed to be waterproof.

"You saved us, Humphrey," Naomi said, patting the dragon's scaly side.

"Yeah, you did a sonic blast and *didn't* kill anyone," said Soraya.

"I didn't like that place," said Humphrey nervously. He was drooling like crazy. "It seems like those pirates *really* didn't want anyone to find the treasure. Why would they be so mean?"

"In *their* minds, it wasn't mean," Soraya said. "They wanted to protect their treasure."

"I still think it's mean," Humphrey muttered. "No one needs a stalactite falling on their head."

Christoff poured water out of his backpack, too, and decided to leave his soggy bag lunch behind.

They marched on down the hall, which luckily was wide enough for Humphrey. Soraya kept her eyes open for more booby traps. She felt exhausted.

"Thank *goodness* my parents got me swimming lessons last year," Naomi said. "I didn't know how to swim before that. But now, my dad and I go swimming all the time."

Soraya's stomach tightened in a way that had nothing to do with booby traps. She *knew* it! "You do?"

"Yeah," Naomi said. "Swimming is our favorite thing to do. You should come with us sometime."

Soraya felt as if she might burst. "I bet your dad is really proud you like science, too, huh?"

Naomi turned around and looked at Soraya, her brows crinkling together. "Yeah, he is. Why?"

Soraya balled her fists without meaning to. With all the excitement, she'd actually managed to forget about her family. But now Soraya remembered how different she was from Naomi and Christoff.

She had already guessed it: of *course* Naomi had a perfect life, with a perfect dad who'd never leave her. Naomi was a great student, and nice to everyone, and never said weird things in class.

Soraya was sure that Christoff had a perfect family too. How else could he wear lederhosen to school without worrying what anyone would say?

Soraya stopped walking. She sat on the tunnel floor and dropped her head down over crossed arms.

"Soraya." Christoff stopped walking too. "What's wrong? Aren't you coming?"

She looked at the ground. "You just want to be my friend because I met a dragon. Or, you just want to find the treasure."

"Actually, we wanted to be friends before all this," Naomi said. "No offense, Humphrey. You're amazing too."

Humphrey blinked. "I'm amazing?" He puffed out his dragon chest a little.

"We like you, Soraya," Christoff said. "You've always got something interesting to say. Plus, you know all about portals and pirates."

"You wouldn't like me if you really knew me," Soraya said shortly. "My dad's gone. And my mom thinks I'm too weird and she wishes I was normal."

She flushed as soon as she said it. They'd never want to be friends with her now.

"Well, your mom's wrong about that," said Christoff. "Being normal is boring. I'd much rather be weird." He stuck his thumbs under the suspenders of his lederhosen and struck a pose.

"Me too," said Naomi, smiling at Christoff's silliness.

A little smile crept onto Soraya's face too. As she giggled at Christoff's antics, a long-forgotten memory flashed into her mind. It was before her dad had left, and she must have been really little. She was dressed in a colorful cape, striking superhero poses and laughing. And . . . her mom was there. Also dressed in a colorful cape and laughing.

That can't be right, she thought. Her mom never did anything that fun.

Soraya shook off the memory. She didn't have time to think about this right now. Instead, she studied Christoff and Naomi in the beam of her penlight.

Could she trust them? The way she had trusted Estelle?

Soraya's forehead wrinkled. If one person really and truly liked her—and Estelle did, she knew that—maybe, just maybe, Christoff and Naomi could too.

Her mind reeled. What would it be like to have friends? People to hang out with, eat lunch with, and sit with on the bus?

Before Soraya could say anything else, Humphrey called back to them from the end of the tunnel. "I think I see something up here," he said. "Come look at this, guys."

They hurried up behind him. Soraya aimed her light into the cavern opening. Beyond it was a beautiful space full of pale stalactites and stalagmites. They were so smooth and shiny she realized they were wet.

It was so pretty that Soraya was temporarily distracted from the thoughts she'd just been having.

"It's a palace," she said. "These rock formations are like towers."

"It *does* look like a castle!" said Naomi, wandering around.

Soraya pulled out the treasure map. She and Christoff squinted at it. "This room's not on the official cavern map, but it *is* on this treasure map," he said. "The pirates named it the Music Room." He glanced across the space. "According to the pirate map, we're supposed to go through a tunnel over there. I don't see an opening, though. Maybe Humphrey could try to blast it open?"

Soraya shook her head. "No . . . the pirates will have left a clue somewhere. I'm sure there's a trick to get through this room."

"What's this?" Soraya pointed at the map. Next to the Music Room on the page, there was a tiny drawing that looked kind of like a hammer. Next to it were written the letters C, C, G, G, A, A, G. "That's got to be a clue."

"Look!" Christoff ran to the nearest stalagmite and picked up a mallet that had been placed at the base of the rock. "It's that hammer on the map—it's actually a mallet! It looks like the ones that play the stalactite organ."

"But what do those letters on the map mean?" said Naomi. "C, C, G, G, A, A, G?"

Christoff looked around the room, and back at the mallet. "They're musical notes, I think!" he exclaimed. "Musical notes have letter names from A to G."

"Do you think there's another stalactite organ hidden in here somewhere?" said Naomi.

"No," Christoff said. "I think it's something else. I wonder . . ." He took the mallet and tapped it on the side of a stalactite.

A sweet, soft sound rang through the room.

Humphrey wiped his eyes. "Beautiful. I love music. The bats told me my dragon parents used to sing to me when I was an egg."

Christoff wandered around, tapping on different stalactites. Each one made a different sound. "I think we're supposed to play the notes on the map, in the right order. That's how to get through this room."

"Christoff knows a ton about music," Naomi explained. "He plays the tuba in band. The band director said he has something called perfect pitch."

"We just need to find the rock formations that produce the right notes," Christoff said.

He tapped the sides of several more stalactites. "What's the first note I need?"

Soraya glanced at the map. "C. And then another C."

Christoff went around, tapping and listening while Soraya read him the letter for each note. Sometimes he smiled when he found a note. Sometimes he frowned and muttered to himself.

"We don't have long," Naomi said, glancing at her watch. "Less than an hour to get to the gift shop."

Finally, Christoff nodded in satisfaction. "I've got it! Listen."

He hurried around the room, tapping the stalactites to make notes in order of the letters on the map. Soraya didn't know musical notes, but they sounded enchanting. And she recognized the song—"Twinkle, Twinkle, Little Star."

The minute Christoff hit the last note, a huge hidden door slid open. It was even big enough for Humphrey.

"Yay!" Humphrey cried. "I don't have to melt anything!"

"I knew you could do it, Christoff," said Naomi. Christoff took a bow.

They all headed for the door, but Soraya stopped just before she reached it.

"Watch out, guys," she said nervously. "Be careful. There still may be booby traps."

She flashed her penlight on the ground, which looked solid enough.

Holding their breaths, they shuffled through the door. Humphrey let out a huge sigh of relief.

And then the floor opened up underneath them, and they tumbled into the darkness.

Reunion

As they tumbled and rolled, Soraya was glad Humphrey wasn't right above her. He was somewhere below, howling. Every once in a while, a speck of drool flew past her face.

They were skidding down some kind of wide slide, like a chute made of rock.

Finally, they stopped falling. Humphrey landed first. Everyone else landed on top of him.

"Ooomph." With a thud, Christoff bounced off Humphrey's back. "Sorry, Humphrey."

Naomi and Soraya slid off Humphrey. Soraya stood up, her legs wobbly, and shined her penlight on all of them. Once she'd confirmed that no one was hurt, she focused on their surroundings. This was the deepest, darkest place they'd been in so far—they seemed to be at the bottom of a pit. The walls around them were high and steep. She couldn't even see the ceiling, which was somewhere way, way up in the drafty darkness.

"I don't like this place," Naomi whispered. She was shining her flashlight around, too.

Soraya shivered in her wet clothes. "Let's get out of here as fast as we can."

"Good idea," said Christoff, wide-eyed. "*This* definitely isn't on the official cavern map."

"What's that sound?" said Humphrey.

There was an intense rumbling. The earth shook under their feet. The walls around them started to shake, too.

"Is it an earthquake?" Naomi cried, as pebble-sized bits of rock began raining down on them.

"Either an earthquake or another booby trap." Soraya yelped as a pebble bounced off her forehead. "Either way, we've got to get out of here!"

Humphrey waddled between them, drooling all over the floor. He opened his wings and spread them over the others.

"At least this'll help a little," he said.

"But what about you?" said Soraya. "Don't the stones hurt you?"

"Dragon hide is tough," he said.

Soraya huddled up to him. "What are we going to do now?"

Humphrey took a deep breath. His voice trembled. "I have an idea, but it's a little crazy."

"There are no crazy ideas at a time like this!" said Christoff, who was huddled against Humphrey's other side.

"All right." Humphrey took another deep breath. He was drooling again. "You'll have to get out from under my wings and climb on my back."

"Is your plan going to work?" Soraya said.

"I don't know," Humphrey said. "But I have to try."

"Whatever it is, I think it's a good idea," said Naomi.

Soraya hesitated. She didn't like the idea of climbing on Humphrey's back, right under the falling stones. But Nimbla Moony would tell her to trust her friends.

Soraya felt a strange pang. Did that mean these were her friends?

Yes. They were. And she could trust them.

"Let's go, guys!" she said, and dashed out from under Humphrey's wings.

Right away the pebbles rained down on them, pinging onto their heads and shoulders. Humphrey crouched down so that it was easier for them to scrabble up his back. They sat in a row right between his wings.

"The rocks are getting bigger!" said Naomi, shielding herself from the raining stones.

"Hold on tight," Humphrey said.

He lifted his head, breathed deep, and started beating his wings. He beat once, beat twice—and then began to lift off the ground. He bobbed up and down so much that Soraya had to hold on with all her might.

"I haven't flown in a long time," he said, his voice shaking.

"You're doing great," said Christoff.

Humphrey opened his mouth, and let out a sound that gave Soraya chills all the way to her bones—he *roared*. It was louder than a speeding train. It was deeper and stronger than the roars of the lions she'd seen at the zoo. It echoed off the walls of the pit.

Naomi, who was behind Soraya, gripped her around the waist.

Humphrey beat his wings harder and started flying straight up, careening past falling stones. When a big stone headed for them, he drew back his head—and then a sonic wave burst from his mouth, blasting the stones into pieces.

"Whoa, Humphrey," Soraya said. "Amazing!"

Humphrey whimpered. "It's scary to do that."

"Keep going, Humphrey!" said Christoff as he dodged a rock.

Soraya looked around, still clutching her penlight. She realized the walls weren't actually sheer—there were little ledges in some places. And on every ledge, something littered the dark ground.

Bones.

"Are those *skeletons*?" asked Naomi.

Soraya shuddered. "They must be the bones of people who tried to find the treasure before us, and failed."

"There are old pickaxes and ropes by some of them," said Christoff. "They tried to climb the walls."

Drool flew past Soraya's face. "I don't like bones," wailed Humphrey.

He dodged more rocks, streaking along. Soon the ceiling was right above them, filled with stalactites as sharp as fangs. And in front of them was a stone door in the wall, right under the ceiling.

The stone door was shut.

Humphrey hovered there, beating his wings.

"What do we do now?" he said, as the fangs above them trembled.

Christoff steadied himself on the dragon's back and unrolled the treasure map. "Humphrey, it looks like the bat area is right on the other side of that door."

Humphrey beat his wings even faster. A long strand of drool (it seemed to be excited drool this time) dangled from his mouth. "My *family* is in there? But how will we get through?"

"Humphrey," said Naomi, "you've been sonic-blasting those falling stones, right?"

"Yes," said Humphrey in a small voice.

"I think you need to sonic-blast this door," said Soraya.

"But that will be a way bigger blast! What if I hurt someone?"

The ceiling trembled again, dangerously. Stones were still falling on them.

"If you *don't* try it," said Christoff, "we may end up like those piles of bones down there."

Humphrey took a deep breath. "Soraya, will you hold my hand?"

"I can't, I'm on your back," she said. "But I can hold your ear, if that helps."

"That helps," Humphrey said, as Soraya grabbed hold of his ear.

His face scrunched up. And then he opened his mouth.

An enormous force shot out of it, right at the rock—which blasted into pieces.

Soraya closed her eyes. She was still clutching Humphrey's ear. She blinked her eyes open and looked around. There was dust everywhere, but there were also—bats!

Right away they were swarmed with bats. Hundreds and hundreds of them flew out of the hole in the wall.

A few of them shrieked when they saw Humphrey.

"Humphrey! *Humphrey!*" They zoomed toward his face. *"Humphrey's back!"*

Humphrey drooled and wept and smiled and looked as if he might die of happiness.

"My friends!" he said. "Come on, I want you to meet my bat parents!"

He flew through the blasted-open hole into the bat area, which was enormous. Soft light filtered in from above, so they could see without flashlights. It was like its own world. Beautiful stalactites, stalagmites, and other formations grew everywhere. Some of the spires were long and spindly, like the high turrets of castles. Some were low and stout, and looked like fairies' homes. And everywhere, there were flowing formations that looked like water, as if waterfalls gurgled all over a little kingdom. The ceiling was high here, so there was plenty of space to fly.

Humphrey landed. He was sobbing now. "Home. I'm home!"

Soraya, Naomi, and Christoff slid off his back.

Two bats fluttered over to them, squeaking loudly.

"Could it be our boy?" one of them said, screeching. "Is that Humphrey?"

"Mama Bat! Papa Bat!" said Humphrey. "Yes, it's me!"

They glided down and hugged his huge neck with their little wings, chattering loudly. Humphrey bawled and hugged them back.

The other bats swarmed over and hung upside down from Humphrey's arms, his wings, even his dragon-y beard. Soraya wrinkled her nose at a sharp smell wafting through the space.

"Guano," whispered Naomi. "Bat poop. You get used to it."

Soraya wanted to ask Naomi how many times in her life she'd smelled bat poop, but instead she hung back, overwhelmed with a million emotions. She imagined her own dad running toward her like this, his arms open wide, and the lump formed in her throat again.

At the same time, she was so happy to see Humphrey smiling.

"Soraya, Naomi, Christoff, this is my adoptive mama and papa," Humphrey said. His whole body trembled with tears. "They took care of me when I was just a baby, and taught me everything they know."

"You have a beautiful place here," said Christoff.

"Nice to meet you," said Naomi.

"Humphrey is one brave dragon," added Soraya, trying not to worry that Humphrey would forget her, now that he had his bat family back.

"That he is," said Mama Bat, squeaking. She poked Humphrey with her wing. "Where have you *been*?"

"It's a long story." Humphrey settled down on his haunches, and started telling the bats what had happened.

Naomi turned to Soraya and Christoff and whispered, "The treasure. It's supposed to be in this room, right?"

Christoff had already gotten the map out and was bent over it. "Yup." Then he shook his head.

"What is it?" said Soraya.

"There's tiny writing here. It says that to find the treasure, we'll need to solve a riddle."

9

The Best Treasure Ever

"This is turning out to be a pretty intense adventure," said Christoff, his belly rumbling. "I could go for a snack."

"Never mind that!" said Naomi. "What's the riddle?"

Soraya pulled the map close to her face and squinted. "It says, '*When I change, I make a loud sound. I get bigger but weigh less. What am I?*'" She frowned. "I hate riddles. I'm no good at them."

Naomi scrunched up her face. "I have no idea what that could be."

Christoff tapped his forehead and glanced at his watch. "I don't either. But we have to figure it out *soon*. Our class will be in the gift shop in less than half an hour. And did I mention I'm starving?"

"Hmmm." Soraya looked around to see if she could find any more clues. Nimbla Moony had so many superpowers and gadgets. She never had to rely on riddles to figure anything out. If she were here, she'd just use her Universal Detection Device to find the treasure.

Soraya felt another sudden pang. She remembered that her dad had liked riddles. When she was really little, he used to practice them with her.

She tried to push the thought out of her mind, but thinking about her dad always left her feeling shaky.

"What makes a loud sound when it gets bigger?" mumbled Soraya, as her eyes scanned the cavern. Then she whirled around and pointed. "I've got it! Christoff, Naomi, look at that rock formation over there."

Christoff forgot about food and jumped up. "What about it?"

Soraya beamed. "The shape. What does it remind you of?"

"It looks like a bunch of white, bumpy things in a pile," said Naomi. "Just like . . ."

"Popcorn!" said Christoff. His stomach was still growling.

"Exactly," said Soraya. "That's what makes a loud sound when it changes. It gets bigger and weighs less." She started running toward the rock formation. Naomi and Christoff followed. Even Humphrey waddled behind them.

Naomi knelt at the foot of the rock formation and started feeling around it. "I can't believe it—there's a *button*."

Soraya dropped to her knees. There *was* a button, right in the stone.

"Push it," said Christoff.

The bats and Humphrey gathered behind her. Everyone held their breath as Soraya pushed the button. For a moment, nothing happened. Then, the giant stone started to rumble—and a little door opened at its base.

She couldn't see what was inside—it was too dark.

"A magic door," Humphrey whispered. "This was here the whole time. We never knew!"

"The pirates built this." Soraya reached into the hole with shaking hands. Her fingers grasped something solid, with straight sides.

With a grunt, she pulled out the heavy object.

"A *treasure* chest," said Christoff.

He was right. It was a real treasure chest, like the ones in pirate movies. Soraya's heart pounded. She set it down on the ground.

"You should be the one to open it, Soraya," Humphrey said in a trembling voice. "This whole quest was your idea."

Soraya could hardly breathe as she opened the lid of the chest.

She gasped. She'd expected to find jewels and gold. Instead, nestled inside the box were . . . three *eggs*? Giant, colorful, scaly eggs, each one almost as big as her head.

Humphrey let out a little cry. He gently picked one of them up in his claws.

"Dragon eggs!" he said. "These are *dragon eggs*!"

"There's a note." Christoff reached into the chest. He pulled out a wrinkled old piece of paper, and held it toward the light. "It says, '*I've hidden these eggs until a worthy soul finds them. They've been waiting for the right person— or creature—to take care of them. They won't hatch until they're brooded with love.*'"

Humphrey picked up all three eggs. He carried them to a little groove between stalagmites, and placed them inside. "They'll need to stay warm until they hatch," he said anxiously. Then he settled his entire huge body on top of them.

Soraya winced. She expected to hear shells cracking any second. But there was no sound of the eggs breaking.

"Dragon eggs must be pretty tough," said Naomi, shaking her head with relief.

"You're going to be a dad, Humphrey!" said Christoff. "How does it feel?"

Humphrey's eyes filled up. "I always wanted to be a dad."

The bats flitted around excitedly, squeaking and screeching, diving down to get a glimpse of the eggs.

"You're the best dragon in the world to have your own babies," said Soraya. "You'll be a great dad, Humphrey."

She felt another twist of her heart as she said this. She knew it was true. Humphrey would love his eggs. He would never leave them, if he could help it.

Naomi glanced at her watch. She leapt to her feet. "We only have a few minutes to get to the gift shop!"

"That tunnel opening over there leads to the tourist part of the cavern," said one of the bats, squeaking. "But the passage is blocked by a barred metal door. They locked it when they sealed off this area. We can fly through the bars to visit other parts of the cave, but tourists can't come in here anymore."

"So that's where we need to go," Soraya said grimly. "We don't have a key, though."

"There's no key, but there's a keypad." Naomi was already at the door, examining it. "We just have to guess the code. It's a letter keypad, so the code will be a word."

"Hmm . . . try spelling the word CAVERN," Christoff suggested.

Naomi tried it. No luck.

"What about UNDERGROUND?" said Soraya.

Nothing.

"Wish we could help, but we don't know the code either," said one of the bats.

"What about EGG?" suggested Humphrey.

Nope.

They kept guessing and guessing, until finally Soraya said, "I know! Try STALACTITE ORGAN."

Naomi tried it. Sure enough, there was a click, and the door sprang open.

"Thank *goodness*," said Christoff. He ran back over to Humphrey and gave him a hug. "Goodbye, Humphrey. It was wonderful to meet you."

Naomi joined him. "Yeah, you're the best, Humphrey."

Soraya hugged him last. She thought about how, just a few hours ago, she hadn't known him at all. Her eyes were full of tears now, too.

"Are you going to forget me?" she asked, her voice muffled.

"Of course not," Humphrey said. "You rescued me! You're an honorary member of our bat and dragon family."

Soraya looked at him. She realized he wouldn't forget her. He had never forgotten his family and friends. He had thought about them every day, had tried to come back to them. And she knew he would always do the same for his eggs.

She wiped her nose. "I won't forget you either, Humphrey," she said, sniffling. "Take good care of your eggs."

"We'll help!" said Mama Bat and Papa Bat. "Baby dragons are a handful, you know."

Humphrey tried to stay very still on his eggs while he hugged her. "You'll come back to visit me, Soraya?"

"*Definitely*," she promised. "And next time, I won't need a map."

"Soraya, we've only got five minutes to make it to the gift shop!" said Christoff.

Soraya watched the bats fussing over Humphrey and his eggs, flying around and hanging from his ears and wings. Just then, an idea for her next comic popped into her head. A comic about a dragon becoming a dad . . .

Soraya turned and raced with Naomi and Christoff through the metal door. They made sure it was closed and locked from the other side, then hurtled through more tunnels toward the main cavern.

Behind them, she could hear Humphrey singing "Twinkle, Twinkle, Little Star" to his eggs.

Swamp Creatures

Naomi, Christoff, and Soraya skidded into the main cavern.

"The gift shop is this way!" said Christoff, leading them up and down ramps. He darted through some beautiful parts of the cavern Soraya hadn't seen yet.

He stopped short at the crowded gift shop, and they all nearly bumped into one another.

Christoff scanned the room. All their classmates were there, milling around the store.

"Where's Ms. Staples?" he whispered.

"Over there." Naomi pointed at their teacher, who was at the register paying for something. "She's too busy to notice we just came in, thank goodness."

Soraya stiffened, suddenly afraid. It was one thing for Christoff and Naomi to act like her friends while they were looking for treasure. But what about in front of their class? Would they pretend not to know her?

"Just try to look as if we've been here all along," said Christoff.

"Come on, Soraya," said Naomi, taking her hand.

"What *happened* to you three?" a voice said.

Soraya whirled around. It was Katie and Madison, Katie 2.0. Their hair was as shiny as ever, and their clothes were as pink as ever. And they were looking at Naomi, Christoff, and Soraya with horrified expressions.

Soraya looked down at herself, then at Christoff and Naomi. All three of them were wet and covered in dirt. On top of that, Christoff had a bit of dragon drool hanging from his ear, Naomi had drool on her sleeve, and Soraya's pant leg was ripped at the knee. Streaks of soot covered their faces.

Soraya, Christoff, and Naomi looked at one another and started to laugh. They howled so hard they couldn't stop.

Katie grimaced. "What's so *funny*? I wouldn't be laughing if *I* looked like that."

"Yeah." Madison twirled her hair around her finger. "You guys look like swamp creatures."

Christoff whooped so hard he staggered backward and knocked a book off a shelf. Soraya bent down to pick it up.

"Hey, look," she said, showing the cover to Naomi and Christoff.

The book was called *Legends of Balabrook Caverns*. There was a picture of a pirate on its cover.

"Maybe you should read this book, Katie," said Christoff.

"Whatever," Katie said. "Have fun being weird."

"We will!" Naomi said, as Katie and Madison turned on their heels and walked away.

Soraya glanced at Christoff and Naomi, who were still laughing. She felt shy all over again, but in a different way this time. She realized that even though they had been hanging out for only a few hours, they had seen her real self.

They had seen her scared, and mad, and sad. They had seen her doubtful and impatient, and had listened to her wild ideas. And yet for some mysterious reason, they hadn't left.

They still wanted to be her friends, even though they had seen all that. Maybe *because* they had seen all that.

Her mom would jump up and down at this news. She would definitely tell Soraya to bring her new friends home for dinner. And Christoff and Naomi were human, which would be a big plus in her mom's book.

Friends were tricky. Anything could go wrong. But… Soraya thought about Humphrey, alone in that cave for so long. She knew he would do anything for his friends, even new friends. Maybe he was right, and friends were worth the risk.

Soraya squared her shoulders and steeled herself. Nimbla Moony would say to be brave.

Soraya imagined the three of them trooping into her perfectly normal beige living room, covered in dragon drool, and her mom fainting on the beige couch.

"Guys, I have a question," she said. "Do you like lasagna?"

Humphrey the dragon says goodbye to his new friends.

Good luck hatching the eggs.

Thanks, Soraya! Come visit soon!

It turns out that egg hatching is harder than it looks.

Okay, gotta keep them warm.

Don't crush them, Humphrey!

Scoot a little to the left!

Salima Alikhan

has been a writer and illustrator for fifteen years. She lives in Austin, Texas, where she is also a college English and creative writing professor. When she went on school field trips as a child, she liked to imagine what sorts of creatures might be lurking in some of those fun places. She wrote stories and drew pictures about those creatures, and loves that she still gets to do that.

ILLUSTRATOR,
SORAYA & THE DRAGON

Atieh Sohrabi

was born and raised in Tehran, Iran, and currently lives in New York City with her family. She started her career in industrial design before switching to a new path in illustrations. Her first illustrated book, published in 2002, received first prize in the 5th Tehran International Biennale Illustration. Since then, her books have appeared in exhibitions and museums around the world, winning numerous international awards.

ILLUSTRATOR,
"HUMPHREY HATCHES HIS EGGS"

Jennifer Naalchigar

is an illustrator based in Hertfordshire, England. She has a love for quirky characters and funny stories and enjoys experimenting with digital brushes. Jen can often be found doodling with her tablet in her local coffee shop. She also enjoys reading picture books to her daughter. She works in children's and educational publishing.

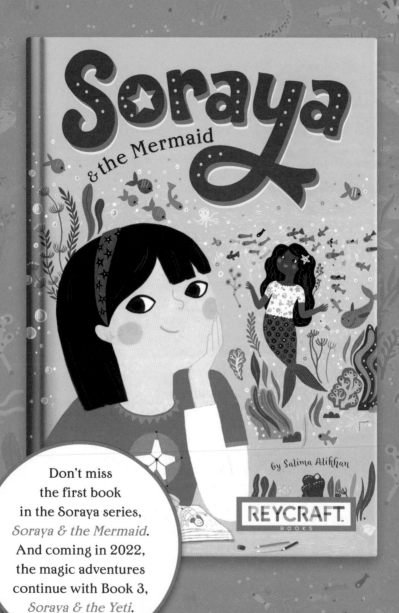

Don't miss the first book in the Soraya series, *Soraya & the Mermaid*. And coming in 2022, the magic adventures continue with Book 3, *Soraya & the Yeti*.